EAU DE PARFUM

HELL IN A HANDBAG: ERIC'S STORY SHORT

LISA ACERBO

TG Publishing Partners, LLC

CONTENTS

BLURB: EAU DE PARFUM

The smell of Streaker lingers in the air.

I must be dead!

I woke up naked and covered in blood. Teeth marks littered my arms, creating holes and revealing muscle. Someone or something attempted to gnaw off my elbow.

I'm alone! So, maybe, I'm worse than dead.

If friends and family abandoned me, I must have turned into a Streaker. On second thought, it's an easy "no" to eating body parts.

The idea of brains for dinner disgusts me.

I only see one option ahead, and that's to find my family and ask why they left me as dinner for the undead.

Eau De Parfum
HELL IN A HANDBAG
Eric's Story Short
COPYRIGHT©2021
Lisa Acerbo
Cover Design by Wren Taylor

Published in the United States of America by:
DLG Publishing Partners
PO Box 17674

San Antonio, TX 78217

www.DLGPublishingPartners.com

WAKING THE DEAD

His glance was quick and furtive. Nostrils flaring, Eric recoiled from the gore around him and the smell of death saturating the air. He held back a scream.

Where am I?

The irregular beat of his heart pounded in his ears like a truck accelerating under a bridge. Although the room was murky, the red ochre stains decorating the floor and walls like abstract paintings remained vivid.

What had happened here?

Eric sat naked, covered in blood, but alive. He lifted himself onto his knees. Everything hurt. He stared at the carnage that was his body and gagged.

Teeth marks littered his arms, creating holes and

revealing muscle. Someone or something had attempted to gnaw off an elbow. The tears in his thigh reached bone. Eric yanked his hand to cover the wound then tore it away. Half-healed scabs and open sores covered from fingers to wrist.

Is this what it's like to be dead? How long have I been here? Like this?

Memories surged back to him. A few days ago, he and the rest of the survivors had taken refuge in this old movie theater, but Streakers found them.

The maggoty swarm had assembled along the large glass windows and doors. Agitated, held back from their sustenance, the zombies writhed and swayed against the barrier.

Dead eyes had stared from outside. Decayed, naked bodies, twisted limbs, peeling skin, and pustules, the Streakers blurred into a mirage of rot and decay. Many lacked clothes, leaving everything that hadn't decomposed dangling in the open air.

His friends, Jenna and Caleb, had tried to herd Eric and his twin brother, Billy, to safety, but he'd pushed them away. Nearly sixteen, he had wanted to prove himself.

The shattering window had left him frozen in fear. One of the zombies focused its lifeless eyes on him.

A sound? Eric's thoughts rushed into the present.

Quiet.

What happened to his friends? Had they all perished? Worse, had they abandoned him?

The crunch and crackle of broken glass had Eric jumping to his feet and heart thumping against his ribs. Adrenaline flooded aching limbs into action.

Frantic, he searched the ground for a weapon but found nothing. He sprinted, pain in each step, to the corner and waited. There was little else to do.

The thing moved toward him. An atrocity Eric smelled from a distance over his own unpleasant scent. As the figure emerged from the shadows, he recognized a human face covered with tufts of matted hair.

A long, unkempt beard hid already thin lips. More hair, in knotted dread-like tangles ascended from the scalp and cascaded in all directions. Twigs had lodged in the mess, and Eric had an absurd vision of a bird springing out of the tangled dread-locks like an animated character in an old-fashioned Disney movie.

Before him stood a man, not a Streaker. Despite being in much better condition than Eric, his appearance indicated life had not been kind, but that's the downside of the zombie apocalypse. Life had not been good to anyone of late.

The hairy beast of a man pointed. "What happened to you?"

Eric's mouth dropped open, but words failed. A shy teen again, he tried to find a place in the room to conceal his nakedness from the man's critical scrutiny. Finding nothing to shelter him other than darkness, he squeezed back into the shadows.

"Hello?" The man prompted. "What are you doing in this place?"

"I don't remember what happened, or why I'm here alone." Eric's voice was deep and scratchy, sounding little like he had remembered.

The stranger brandished a glinting crowbar. Eric slipped deeper into the recesses of the dark, abandoned movie theater until the wall pinched his scabbed back.

Nothing I can do to protect myself, but with these wounds I'll be dead soon anyway.

The stranger took a step closer. In addition to the crowbar, a lethal curved sword hung from the belted loops of torn, stained jeans encasing the man's long legs. A bandana encircled his neck, but Eric noticed scars slithering from side to side that the grungy t-shirt with an ironic smiley face couldn't hide. Eric watched the man swing the crowbar with muscular arms, ready to deliver a deadly blow if needed.

Would this be how he died? I'm not ready.

Eric turned his head in a desperate search for an escape route.

"Wait, Kid. Don't get scared. I haven't come across another human for months now, but you look worse than the undead. Shit, are you even human?" The man scratched at the untamed beard with his free hand.

Eric nodded. "Think so. I feel horrible and very human."

The stranger looked like a magician out of a fantasy novel, but this man was no wizard. No magic or spell could ever make this world right again.

Long beats of silence followed. Then, the nameless man set the crowbar on the ground and slid his backpack off. The rifle strapped to the top shone with care.

Eric was sure the weapon was loaded and ready for use.

"I travel light Kid, so don't expect a choice, but you need some clothes." He rummaged through the pack. "Here's my spare t-shirt and jeans. I don't have extra shoes, but I'm sure you will find some if you live long enough."

"Who are you? What happened to my brother, Billy? Where's Jenna and my friends?" Unanswered questions spilled out of his mouth and frantic thoughts pinged across his mind.

The man shrugged, handing over the garments covered in food, grease, and dirt.

Eric took them without hesitation, grateful. He stood and pulled on the shirt first, stumbling as he fought the jeans, and leaned against the wall for support.

"My name's Abraham, but people used to call me Abe. We appear to be the only two idiots crashing this movie theater tonight. I didn't notice any people, living ones, in my travels. There's definitely no one in this town unless you're a fan of the undead. They're everywhere, so keep your voice down."

"Yesterday?" Eric scratched his cheek with bloody fingers. "I think it was yesterday. Maybe the day before. I don't know. We were all in this theater. Are they all gone?"

"You and me. That's it. What's your name?"

"Eric." He scowled, memories of the recent days foggy and ran a hand through his blond hair. Halfway back it stuck to a matted clump, thick and chunky, sticky with what he hoped was blood and nothing worse. Wrenching the hand away, he choked back a gag.

"Sit down, Kid. You're in rough shape. Pray you're not changing into one of them. I'd have to put you down then."

"I'd want that." Eric sat.

Abe followed, his gaze unwavering. "What do you remember?"

"There were sixteen of us traveling together. We were heading to this inn in Virginia. It was supposed to be safe, but we got stuck in this movie theater one day. Lots of undead."

"Sixteen. That's a large group these days."

"Good people. My family. Humans and some of the New Race."

Was he revealing too much?

"New Race, huh? That what you call them"

"They're different but in a good, good way." He stuttered, stuck on exactly how to explain his former companions. "They don't like the light."

"You'd say that's the biggest difference" Abe chuckled. "Been around long enough that I've been introduced to them. Bloodsuckers." Abe massaged his beard. "Sure, they have an allergy to the light, tend to avoid the sun, but the problem is they're stronger than the average person and want to relieve us of our blood, not unlike the undead. Don't like them. Won't travel with them. Surprised your group did."

"They're good and help us survive. Like when we're stuck in here during the day. The front window shattered and Streakers attacked. The New Race defended us but me and my brother Billy had to save Victor when he ventured into the sun." Eric paused, head swarming with bees, pain traveling down his spine. "Jenna tried to get me to go back to safety, but I refused."

"Sounds like they worried about you. How'd you get left here?"

"I don't know." He slapped the ground. "We moved Victor. He's the New Racer I mentioned. Put him in the shadows away from the light. I remember being swarmed by the Streakers but after that, nothing."

"I'm making camp here tonight. If you don't plan to eat me in my sleep, you're welcome to join me."

"I wouldn't ever eat someone." Eric's mouth drew tight.

"A little humor. Relax, Kid. We should move to one of the smaller theaters. I'll patch you up some. I got medical supplies and canned goods. I'm not usually willing to share, but you had a tough day. And it's nice to have company for once. The last interaction I had with humans didn't really end well."

"What happened?"

"I'll tell you more once we're all set in the back. Let's hope for an uneventful evening."

Eric followed Abe through the ruined remains of

the movie theater. The once-grand cineplex was now a chaotic wreck. Bits of plaster mingled with broken furniture. Scattered popcorn containers and crushed candy boxes littered the floor. A detached arm perched on a toppled chair. A few feet away, the torso of a Streakers lay like a statue on the floor. Around the remains, glass covered the floor like the water flooding the beach at high tide.

Eric watched his steps, avoiding the largest, sharp fragments, but they found him, pricking his soles. He must be too far gone to care. The pain no longer registered.

He arrived at the other end of the large lobby, listening for sounds other than his and Abe's footfall. The door to the small theater at the back of the building squealed in rebellion when Abe opened it. Eric waited, weaponless, for anything to jump out, but nothing ventured forth.

Abe grabbed the blade from his belt, then handed over a makeshift weapon.

Eric accepted the crowbar and inched his way into the theater. Heavy in hand, it hurt to lift the weapon. He was thankful when nothing stirred inside.

He stepped deeper into the darkness, Abe's flash-light leading the way.

Silence. Abe stopped, stood motionless, and waved a hand.

What now? How much can I take?

A Streaker sashayed from the shadows as if performing *The Nutcracker* on stage. It limped to the front of the slashed screen,

"Not good," the older man whispered.

Eric closed the gap between him and Abe.

Panic filled Eric when undead, unblinking eyes met his. Dried blood etched a whimsical design on what remained of the zombie's clothing. It shambled forward, stumbling over the wrecked seats in its path, then limped close.

Eric readied himself to fight, palms sweaty, body shaking with fear. He glanced at Abe, who clasped the large, curved sword securely in his huge hands.

The creature lunged at the older man, teeth chomping, the noise loud in the emptiness. Ooze dripped out of blackened lips. The same mold devoured its already gangrenous skin.

In horror, Eric watched the scene unfolding. Abe stepped in front of him, hoisted the blade, and hacked at the zombie that ignored the toppled seats blocking its way.

With each stroke, the creature's outstretched arm dropped lower until, with a thud, the limb hit the ground. The monster, unphased, did not falter, hooked fingers on its still attached hand, reaching for Abe's face. The older man stepped away from the slow-moving Streaker and swung the weapon into its neck, strokes steady as if he had trained for this battle his whole life. The head of the creature flew off its decrepit shoulders and onto the carpet. The headless body swayed briefly, then pitched forward.

Greasy, dark blood decorated the stained carpet.

Eric sank to the ground, weak and nauseous.

"Dinner, anyone?" Abe asked.

"Not funny."

"Sorry, Kid, but being alone for such a long time might have warped my sense of humor a little bit." Abe's scrutiny moved from the Streaker to Eric. "You okay?"

"I'll live." He gave the older man a small smile. "How'd you do that?" He wheezed. "I'm feeling a little out of shape. Even hauling the crowbar has me sucking wind and in need of a nap."

"Ex-military or rather I was in the military until the world collapsed around me."

Eric grunted and huffed in a breath to steady himself, then rose to his feet. He swayed but moved deeper inside the small confines of the theater.

Abe collected the arm he'd hacked off and put it on top of the torso. He bent, picked up the head, and added it to the pile, arranging it to resemble a Basquiat painting.

"Need help?" Eric took a step back.

Please say no.

"That's the spirit." Abe kicked the corpse, unphased from the fight. "I'm good for now. You sit and rest for a couple of minutes. That's an order."

"Thanks." He dropped into one of the remaining upright theater chairs.

Abe sealed the door against any new invaders, sheltering the two for the moment.

"Once I rid us of the remains, I'll clean up those wounds and prepare dinner." He peered into the gloom. "It looks like we weren't the first here. Maybe your friends. There are some Streaker bits closer to the stage." He tromped down the aisle, picked up a foot, and held it in the air for Eric to see. "You hungry?" He didn't wait for a reply. "If you're not up for Streaker toes, I got beans or beans."

"What are you going to do with the body parts?" Eric rested his head against the seat back.

"I'll take them back to the lobby and leave the pieces for the vermin." Abe collected more Streaker bits, moving the largest chunks to the door's entrance. With the body parts assembled, he ventured out of the small theater, hauling the remains.

Eric rose from his seat even though every muscle protested. "Might as well be useful." Lifting a corpse's head by the sandpapery hair, he studied the face for a moment. With a flick of his wrist, he threw it into the corridor. Abe picked it up, grabbed a rubbery leg, and marched off into the main hall, fading into the murk. On his last trip back, he lugged the headless carcass out of the room by its legs.

Returning to the small theater, Abe hauled in an overstuffed backpack. He opened it and brought out extra clothes, cans of food, a small medical kit, and a canteen.

"I stashed near the entrance in case I needed to make a quick escape. Always have a back-up plan, Kiddo."

"I don't have any plans. I don't have anything at all."

"Come here. Let's do something about that."

Eric surveyed his wounds under the dim light of a battery-powered lantern before ripping the shirt Abe handed him, turning it into strips of bandages.

The clear liquid Abe poured on his shoulder and arms burned like battery acid.

"Hey." He ducked his head into the opposite shoulder to hide the words he didn't want Abe to hear. When he turned back, he grunted, "That stings."

"It's just alcohol, boy. I'd say you've been through a lot worse. Hold this." He handed off most of the strips of what was once a shirt.

Abe bound a long, thin piece of fabric around the remaining bits of flesh clinging to Eric's muscle and bone.

Once done with the bandages, Abe offered Eric the canteen. "That's the best I can do. I can't believe you're alive with these wounds and scabs everywhere. Tell me again, how'd this happen?"

"I still don't remember the whole thing, or I'd know what happened to everyone. I'm trying." He took a long gulp of water, sighed in contentment, and handed the canteen back to Abe.

Abe opened a can of beans, filled a plate, splitting it cold between them. The aroma that lit the air made Eric's stomach growl.

"Sorry for the meager meal, but I wasn't expecting guests. I'm here because my supplies ran low, and I needed to restock. Pittsfield was the closest town to the house I stayed in, but it was time to move on. I was getting too much attention from Streakers."

"My group was trying to find a safe place too." He gazed at the older man.

Should I trust him? Abe had helped, possibly saved him. He might as well tell all.

"There was an inn in rural Virginia called the High Point Inn that someone suggested, and we were headed there." Eric paused to see if Abe appeared interested. "That was the plan."

"Sounds like a smart idea." Abe scratched at his bird's nest of a beard. "I was on active duty with the army when the virus broke. My wife and family lived in New Jersey. I lost everyone quick. I didn't even get to tell them goodbye."

"I'm sorry."

"People who made it this long all share the same story these days. No one has any family left."

"I have a twin brother, Billy," he said. "At least I did."

The older man arched an eyebrow. "There weren't any relatively recent, not too decayed remains that looked human around the theater. Maybe everyone escaped."

"It's just as likely the Streakers didn't leave anything to be identified."

"Undead don't usually eat bones."

"The other option is Billy, Jenna, and the rest of them left me here."

"Jenna?"

"A friend. They wouldn't leave me here to die?" His voice cracked.

"I don't believe there are only those two options.

They're either dead or left you. Maybe they went for help. They needed time to rally. The group could be in a nearby building on the way back to fetch you. There has to be another scenario, Kiddo."

"I'm not sure." He covered his eyes with his palms to force back the tears.

2

TRAIN TO GAIN

Eric made a notation on a small pad with a nub of a pencil he sharpened with his pocket-knife. One month had passed since he met Abe in the movie theater. He'd left a note for his brother when they departed the theater, but as days blew away like leaves he had less and less hope he'd catch up with the group or that they would find him.

"Hey, Kid," Abe called to him from the campfire that held back the encroaching shadows. "We have a little while before it gets dark. Want to practice some self-defense moves?"

Abe hadn't taken it easy on Eric. As soon as Abe thought him able, they'd started training with knives, guns, and hand to hand. Eric liked practicing with the knives and guns best. Hand to hand meant he'd be sore when he hit his bedroll. He'd yet to beat Abe at anything.

"Sure." Eric stood and stretched. As much as he hated the beating, it had helped. He'd been feeling better, healing, and more importantly, watching the muscles sprout in his arms and legs. With little food, he'd developed a washboard stomach thanks to all the core work Abe forced him to do.

If only there were women around to notice.

Stashing the pad and pencil in the back pocket of ripped, washed-a-few-weeks-ago jeans, Eric sauntered over to Abe.

Abe jabbed.

Eric ducked under the second swing, stood straight to parry, but a flat palm caught him in the chest at the heart.

"That strike could have taken you out. Don't forget what I taught you so far about Kempo Karate," Abe said. "Focus. Start with a block or parry when a strike comes. Then moving in for a strike. When you do strike, no holding back."

Eric steadied himself in fighting form and waited. Abe held back on purpose, letting long seconds pass by like leaves falling to the ground in slow descent buoyed by the wind. The older man formed his hand as if gripping an orange, waited a beat, and then released the hold. With lightning strike intensity, he jabbed. Eric deflected, stretching out his arm.

Abe jammed his fingers into Eric's outstretched bicep and pincered the muscle, pulling him close. The heel of his other palm smacked into Eric's cheek. "That could have been your nose. I'd have broken it easy."

"I'm letting you win to feel good old man," Eric wheezed.

The words died in his throat when Abe's hand struck his neck and dug into his windpipe, cutting off his air.

"How do you respond?" Abe asked.

Eric gasped, unable to speak. He could move, and threw himself into Abe, sending them both crashing to the ground. Eric landed on top and shot an elbow into Abe's abdomen. Eric enjoyed the grunt of pain.

Abe rolled to the side and struck out at Eric's groin. Eric jerked to the left and balled into the fetal position. He lay still.

"You okay?" Abe asked. "I took it easy on you this time."

Eric coughed a few times and sat up.

Abe helped him stand. "You're improving. When you're ready, we'll practice the moves for a while, and maybe do some calisthenics. Too late for a run tonight, but maybe we start tomorrow off with a run with our packs. Let's say the first ten miles."

"You fight like a girl," Eric said.

Abe laughed. "Fifty pushups, mister."

In the morning, Eric packed quickly, but made sure nothing was overlooked. Abe had trained him well this last month. His backpack, which he organized and repacked often, was filled with supplies and road ready. He lifted it to his shoulders. It felt heavy. He carried the tent, provisions, weapons, and clothes.

Abe still tried to travel light, but the weight of each backpack had increased, and Eric was up for the challenge. Formerly long and lanky, the last month of training built the muscle in his arms, legs, and core. A rubber band curtailed his long, sandy hair. While he no longer bandaged his wounds, the crusty scabs still decorated his body.

Even with his improved physique, the morning run turned out to be a struggle. Eric was sore and tired from the night before, but he kept up, falling behind Abe's leggy jog only a few times.

Abe had kept Eric alive this past month, fending off Streakers, teaching Eric survival skills including foraging for edible wild plants and berries. He'd learned how to hunt small game such rabbits and squirrels. The two even attempted to fish on occasion, adding fresh food and supplementing their canned rations. He had a lot to thank Abe for.

The group he'd travelled with prior viewed Eric as a Kid and sheltered him. Abe saw him as a man. Still, as the day's trek dragged, Eric let the discontent settle around his.

He wanted to be with his family again.

When they'd settled in for the night, Eric helped start the fire, set up the tent, and unrolled his bedding.

Abe went hunting and brought back two squirrels, which they made into stew.

After a meager meal, Eric asked the question that was on his mind all day. "It's probably a stupid thing to go and search for the inn, but I'm at a loss. I miss my brother. We're twins." He thumped his chest. "If he perished, I'd know."

"Kid, we're doing okay just the two of us. We've survived, got some goods, plenty of rations. I'm happy having company. What more is needed? There's not a lot to want in this world? Money. Naw. Drugs. Can't find them. Women. Even less available."

"I want to find my family."

"I consider you my family now."

"You're family, but Billy is my brother" Eric lowered his head.

"Let me think on it."

With that the night was ended. Eric took first watch, Woke Abe after what he thought equaled four hours, and fell into a weary sleep.

The next morning the two made quick work of packing the final pieces of camping equipment. They were on the road long before the sun hit the asphalt. Gear snug against their backs, the duo and marched down the road.

What's ahead of us? Eric wondered. *"If it's not about finding my family?"*

"You might not like what you find," Abe said as if he'd read Eric's mind.

"You're wrong. They wouldn't leave me. My brother would never do that."

"The Lord sent you to me. I found you. It is our destiny to start over and find more holy ones to begin a new world. Wait and see."

"It was dumb luck you found me in the movie theater."

"No." Abe's stare turned intense. "It was destiny. My calling came clear when I I met you. The evils of this new world are vast, but purity still exists. It's in you. God mended your flesh. You should have died from all the wounds or turned into a Streaker, but here you are."

"I really don't want to argue about this." Eric's words were clipped.

The two returned to silence, Eric angered by the fact Abe wouldn't help him and his own fear of venturing out alone. He was stronger, but was he strong enough?

Eric had grown close to Abe in their month together, but Abe refused to agree to help him find the rest of the group, calling it a fool's errand. He stressed how everyone had abandoned Eric, leaving him close to death to save themselves. In Eric's mind, they were now a month farther apart.

Abe did have one valid point. Eric should have been crippled, possibly paralyzed, by the wounds he received in the movie theater. Instead, he was healing and strong. Abe's training had made his body stronger, but fear and doubt lingered in his mind. Nightmares of the movie theater attack in the movie theater continued to disturb him. Streakers, both real and imagined, haunted him.

Eric heard the sounds a moment after Abe had stopped. Abe put a finger to his lips and stepped ahead. He pushed aside the thorny branches of a dense thicket of bushes. A nest of Streakers swarmed like ants.

Terror built bile in his throat. Eric watched, unable to move. The Streakers churned like waves with crazed compulsion. They fed on the corpse of a recently deceased man; the first Eric had seen in his journey with Abe. He lingered for a few seconds, hidden in foliage. The Streakers not only grappled for human remains but tore at each other trying to get closer. Eric, sickened, made his escape, following Abe back into the forest.

They tiptoed first until woods swarmed around him. Clear of death, his breath heaved from spasming lungs. Neither of the men stopped, forcing each other to carefully trod further away. They wouldn't be the Streakers next kill. When Eric stumbled across an access road, he knelt, vomiting his last meal upon the road. Abe dragged him up by the armpit, guiding him back to the highway.

He was thankful when Abe slowed and the two took a break and sat at the edge of the deserted highway. Not so thankful when the two Streakers arrived.

"One for each of us," Abe said.

"You saw what just happened?" By this time, Eric had scavenged his own set of weapons. He stood and swung the bat that he'd personally decorated with nails.

"Pre-game jitters. Show me what you got."

The Streakers wobbled close, and the remains of a tattered button-up shirt flit open revealing the black mold so common on Streaker's skin. Both appeared to be later models, their throat and chest pocked with deep bites and gauges. A Streaker had feasted on them, but not enough to stop the dead from rising.

"I want the one with the big hole in his cheek," Eric pointed the bat at the creature.

"Tweedle Dee and Tweedle Dum," Abe said.

"Who?"

"From *Alice in Wonderland*. Don't you read?"

"Never heard of them."

One of the monsters took a step closer. The other sniffed the air.

"The Cheshire Cat?" Abe frowned.

"Not a clue."

"You're generation astonishes me."

"Gee Dad, I'll try harder."

"Good, let's see you use what I've taught you. I know we've met a few of these on our journey, but you've always been back with the gun. Today you get your hands dirty."

"I'm ready." Eric stepped in front of the creature.

The undead whimpered in its desire for flesh.

"Let's see what you got." He stepped back and swung. The nails embedded into what was left of the undead's cheek. He pulled back, ripping away skin and muscle.

The zombie cared little of the new modification to its face and tried to grab the weapon.

Eric dodged the lumbering monster.

"Stay smart. Just because they're slow doesn't mean they're not deadly. Sometimes they fool you." Abe's knife slashed the Streaker closest to him with repeated jabs.

Eric smashed the bat into the undead's arm. The Streaker ignored it and closed in on him.

Abe, a few steps ahead of Eric, continued to slash. This time across the creature's neck. The monster stretched its arms, and no matter how many strokes of the bat Eric sent to deflect them, they stayed up, fingers groping for his flesh.

"This is a good time for a lesson. I take the Streaker down first, and you have to collect firewood for a week."

"I'm younger and more fit." Eric huffed, already tiring from the repeated swinging of the bat to ward off the zombie.

"I'm training you. I know exactly what you're capable of and I say I have a great shot of winning."

"Deal, Old Man." He focused on the carcass in front of him, lifeless eyes meeting his. "What's the plan?" Eric sidestepped

"Take them down now. Stop lollygagging."

"Lolli...what?"

"Swing the bat."

"Right." Eric swung and then backed away. "No firepower."

"Not this time."

"You're the wise one." Eric took in the creature's battered face. Lines crossed its cheeks and nose, scraping away the humanity. The creature's arms were ribbons on flesh and muscle and yet the undead's eye's met his. "I've seen enough of you."

They faced each other. Eric's arms froze. He forced himself to take a deep breath like Abe taught him. He took another breath and steadied himself.

Aiming for its skull, Eric tried to ignore the pustules that leaked yellow green. He pounded into the monster's flesh until the bat lodged into the hard shell of the skull. He fought through it, bat stroke like a major league player hitting a homerun. The Streaker's gaze never left his until it toppled to the ground.

Eric's hands were covered with the remains of Streaker brain. His bat would be a bitch to clean. "Who won?"

"I think mine went down first," Abe said.

"No way."

"Prove me wrong, Kid."

"I have to collect firewood for a week because you think your Streaker went down first."

"That's the way the cookie crumbles."

"You mean the way the Streaker falls."

Abe laughed. "I like you, Kid."

That night Eric collected firewood for camp and sat down with Abe to discuss a plan. They'd been wandering in the direction of Virginia but needed a way to speed up the process.

The two sat around the roaring campfire, the weather chilly, but not unbearable, and discussed finding the High Point Inn.

"There's no longer internet or phone service so it's not like we can find any GPS coordinates." He drew a picture in the dirt with his finger.

"We're going in the right direction. Not much more we can do."

"There has to be."

"Got any ideas."

"What about maps and atlases? They must still be around. If we find them and study them, I bet we can discover a better, quicker route to Virginia."

Abe hitched his shoulders. "Wasn't any need for them when I traveled alone. Set my own course every day, but I'm not opposed. I don't want to spend a lot of extra time looking for them, but we have to keep scavenging anyway for food and tools and such. Might as well add maps to the list."

"Anything that can get us to my friends as soon as possible." He yawned. "Okay if I sleep first?"

"Sure, I'll wake you in a few."

Eric was sleeping soundly when he heard Abe's growl. "Get up. Visitors."

"This way, friend!" Abe said, leading the lurching and lumbering undead away from the tents but not too far into the darkness. "I think there's only one."

The Streaker trailed Abe like a drunk after a night at the bar. It wore the remains of a ripped, tattered dress that clung to maggoty flesh. Chipped and yellowed buck-teeth protruded from rotting lips.

Eric grabbed his studded bat and ran to Abe's side. "Want help?"

"Why not." Abe stepped back. "Go for it."

Eric connected a couple of weak swings, but they did little against the undead's spongey, already dead and unfeeling skin.

"Put your back into it, Kid."

Before Eric could make another move, fingers connected with the fabric of his hoodie and started to pull him towards an open mouth, yawning large with death.

Panic rushed through him as memories of the movie theater ran through his mind. He froze, not sure what to do next.

"Kid, Jesus, do something. Don't just stand there."

Abe grabbed the bat out of his hand and Eric

heard the crack of wood against bone. The sound repeated as Eric remained rooted. Pus, blood, and skin covered him.

Eric sank to his knees. "I'm sorry. So sorry."

"Don't worry about it, Kid. It just means we have more work to do."

3

WANDERINGS

Days slipped away and a steely chill captured the days. Raw wind hounded Eric and chafed his cheeks but no complaints. He was alive. Maples trees wore red and gold leaves and lounged next to bright scarlet oaks. Long hours of travel gave Eric an opportunity to appreciate the beautiful colors. With the cycle of day and night, he healed.

Late in the day, sun fading, Eric and Abe made camp. He stacked wood in a high pile to feed the fire throughout the night, pitched the tent, and spread out his bedroll.

The warmth of the fire settled into his bones and a yawn escaped. Sleep, he yearned for, but he forced his back stiff and straight. Eric had to stay awake for a four-hour watch.

"You going to make it on watch?"

"Don't I always."

"Want company or prefer to be alone?" Abe hovered, his shadowy figure tall in the dark.

"Can always listen to your stories." Eric picked at a lone scar on the back of his palm.

"You can tell a few of your own."

Eric chuckled. "I guess I can. Tell me how you ended up alone. I want the details. You've shared some things but not that."

"Tonight's your lucky night. I'm ready to share."

"Let's hear it." Eric cracked his shoulders and settled against the rock he used for support.

"At first, my town stuck together. People barricaded themselves in the senior center, but it turned ugly quick once supplies got low. The senior residents who survived the outbreak suffered the most —" Abe's head dropped as his words faded.

"What happened to them?"

They were the first—" Abe lifted his head, face reflecting the horror of the memories. "— tortured by the same people I lived with in town. My neighbors and friends. The elderly were reduced to slaves or worse, and finally killed, in some cases, used for food if there was nothing else to eat."

"No."

"People are less than animals, but they can be worse

than Streakers. Humans, if they deserve that title, made choices, many of them horrific. They threw away God, their beliefs, their humanity, and I was part of it."

"It's awful." Eric shook his head in denial.

"We must have faith in God."

"How can you still reckon there's a God?"

"This event is both our curse and our blessing. We're being punished, but we'll also rise. At least the true believers will. Do you believe?"

"I don't know." Eric pawed at the dirt with a stick.

"That's a much bigger discussion for another day."

"What did you do?"

"I left, set out on my own. If my former friends were able to turn on the elderly, they'd just as likely feed me to the Streakers if they didn't harvest my organs for a meal first."

"My friends aren't like that."

"You'd be surprised. That's how I arrived here alone but alive. I couldn't give a damn what happened to any of the lot."

"You don't care? About anyone?"

"Not after what I witnessed. I care about my own survival. I avoid people I meet because they're usually as evil as the Streakers. You'll see. Those you trust will turn on you. Didn't you say you thought all your friends left you to die?"

"I don't remember what happened, but I don't want to believe that."

The older man nodded. "It's instinct. Kill or be killed. I was pretty much out of supplies when I came to Pittsfield. I broke my self-imposed isolation to find some food. Low-and-behold, I ran into you."

"Dumb luck."

"Destiny. God's hand at work."

You said you don't trust anyone or travel with anyone. Should I be concerned?"

"Nah. I can tell you're different. Haven't been corrupted by all the evil."

Eric focused on the stick drawing he etched on the ground. "My friends are nothing like the people you described." He wanted to prove Abe wrong. "We're a family, and I miss them so much."

"There are times I miss the jerks I was with. Those people weren't always bad. We had backyard picnics and went to church together. My daughters played with their Kids. There's comfort in community, but it's a false comfort when society doesn't have a moral compass. When there aren't any churches, the government's fallen, and chaos rules, people will do whatever to survive."

"Not true. People are good, maybe a little warped

by the end of the world, but not evil. My brother's crazy, but not like deranged crazy."

God, I miss my brother.

"Crazy, huh?" Abe chuckled. "Worse than you?"

"In the best of ways." And Jenna is the best friend imaginable. She's also amazing with a weapon just like Caleb. Gus and Emma act like parents, and I hate it, but we help each other to ensure everyone's safety. I have to find them. They're good people."

"I'm sure you'll find them," Abe pushed off the ground, stood stiff, and straightened. "I'll even stay with you until you find out what happened and why they left, if that's what you want. Got to admit, I'm kind of curious why these so called amazing friends would feed ya to the Streakers and leave ya alone"

"They didn't." Eric shook his head, causing his now washed hair to fly across his eyes. "You would?"

Abe nodded. "Sure, Kid. I'd like to meet this family of yours."

Eric exhaled, shoulders slumping, tension slipping from him. "I was afraid you might want to go your own way."

"Even I'm not cold-hearted enough to abandon a Kid."

"I'm not a Kid." Eric hauled up the stick and dashed it into the ground. "Thanks. We've been traveling together but never talked about what would happen. I wasn't sure if you wanted to partner up or go your own way. I would've missed the company."

Abe moved a few steps away. "Don't embarrass me, boy."

"Wait." Something had been bothering him that he needed to tell Abe even if he sounded insane. "I might have died. But I'm getting better."

Abe's laughter echoed in the emptiness.

Eric huffed and watched the older man's mirthful face turn serious.

"That doesn't make any sense." Abe's lips compressed momentarily. "Only God can bring someone back from the dead."

"I keep thinking back to the moment you found me. It plays over and over in my head every night. I remember the events of the day prior: getting to the movie theater with the group, the Streakers surrounding the place and crashing through the window, even the Streakers surrounding me, and the pain. My mind is blank after that. Nothing until I woke up and met you." He rolled his sleeve, staring into the scars and remaining scabs decorating his arm. Healed and no longer bandaged, they still made him shudder.

"You might have passed out from the injuries or a loss of blood."

"That could be true, but don't you think I should be dead?"

"Be thankful you're alive and still human. Otherwise, staying dead sometimes might be a better option to the alternative."

Eric yawned, exhaustion pouring back into him like cement dumped from a truck. "Maybe, I'm an angel."

"I guess I'd have to be the devil in the scenario." Abe moved close and ruffled the hair on Eric's head. "My tent calls."

Eric stretched out on the cold, hard ground and stared at the sky. He couldn't stifle the loud yawn that exited his lips at the same time he murmured, "Night."

Abe turned, marched back, and dragged him off the ground. "You're worse off than I am. I'll sit here. Go to bed. Be gone with you."

He hustled him off into the tent. "I'm so tired. I don't think a bed of rocks would keep me awake."

"I noticed. You appeared to be falling asleep the moment I stepped away."

Eric dragged himself into the tent and under his bedroll. As soon as his head hit the ground, a deep sleep overtook him.

A dream followed. The cold pierced every point of his body like the gnawing teeth of the Streakers.

The chill of death caused Eric to stiffen. Rigamortis set in. He was unable to move, but out of the death entangling him, came a warm voice he recognized.

"Eric!" It was Jenna.

Black primordial ooze, like oil exploding from under the ground, transformed into demons, surging to life. He attempted to move, to start running towards the voice.

"I'm coming for you. I haven't forgotten. I didn't leave you," Jenna screamed.

He should have been overjoyed, but demons cornered him. Fear overtook.

She moved close. Eric met her gaze, his eyes pleading for help. Instead of his friend, the comatose stare of a Streaker, angry mouth open, exposing a decayed black tongue met him.

The undead grabbed his arm. He heard his skin rip as the monster took a bite. It chewed his flesh with anger and intensity.

Eric screamed.

Abe shook him. "Hey Kid. It's only a dream."

He woke, t-shirt drenched in sweat.

Shuddering, he bolted upright. "It's my friends." Eric forced the sleepiness away, rubbing at his eyes trying to make the Streaker in his head had disappeared. "They're searching for me."

"It was a dream. You okay?"

Eric nodded. He didn't want to explain his dream. Abe obviously didn't believe him.

"Go back to bed now."

Eric rested his head once again on the bedroll and thought.

It was a dream. Still, they may be searching for me, but do I really want them to find me if they're already dead?

Slowly, he sank into an exhausted sleep.

4

GAINS

Eric rose several dreamless hours later and exited the tent in search of Abe.

A thin string of smoke circled the air in light wisps.

"Where'd you get the cigarettes?" Eric asked.

"I've had them for a while." He grabbed the package. "Want one?"

"No." Eric declined with a wave of his hand.

"By the time eighty percent of the population died, not many of the remaining people wanted to kill themselves with cigarettes. They're easy to come by now. I'm celebrating though so I'll risk a case of lung cancer."

"Why?"

"You survived the night. You were sweating bullets after you woke from the dream. I wondered if you had spiked a fever or something." He smiled. "Gave you a fifty-fifty chance of getting out of that bedroll."

"I'm fine." Eric dragged a ratty sweatshirt over his tousled blond hair. "Really good actually. It's great to be out in the sun. Warm today." He paused. "Only 50 percent chance? Ye of little faith."

Was Abe joking?

"Well, the odds are getting better. The first night we met a few months ago I gave you less than a ten percent chance of living through the next morning."

"Thanks for the vote of confidence. Every day makes me better, stronger. That's got to be a good sign. No lingering effects."

"Must be all the karate moves I'm teaching you."

Eric mimicked a front uppercut right punch. After three months, he was gaining the prowess of an athlete, long and lean. Although scars littered his body, especially his arms, it was easy to see how miles of trekking and daily practice with weapons had created a powerful soldier against the undead. "Do I look any more mature? I feel it."

"Your still a Kid in my eyes, but they've seen things no one should see for many years. You're innocent to that and it makes you young."

"I've seen things too."

"And now you're prepare to deal with them, at

least physically. I don't think anyone truly deals with all this shit on an emotional level. We'd all be crazy then."

"The self-defense and target practice has helped, but it's something else."

"Whatever it is, it's good. Let's get ready to head out. I've been going easy on you, but if you plan on keeping up, you're going to have to train harder. You've got some basics down, but I can't always protect you, and I haven't stayed alive this long caring for strays. I need to know you got my back if I'm going to help you find your people." He snubbed the cigarette out on the ground.

"I'm good. Ready to tackle the day and whatever training you throw my way." Eric lifted his arms and flexed.

Abe started packing, grabbing the few items scattered overnight and shoving them into his decrepit canvas duffle bag. "Tell me about the nightmare. You were mumbling about your friends searching for you and screaming about Streakers."

Eric tore down the tent. "It's all kind of a big jumble in my head," he said, pausing to remember. "I was dreaming about Streakers and the movie theater, but something more familiar too. There were demon things." He rubbed his forehead with his knuckles. "It was just a dream."

"You've been having a lot of them. Maybe it's a calling."

"Not sure what you mean. I heard Jenna's voice in my nightmare. Maybe they're trying to find me. Maybe I want them to be and I'm projecting in my sleep. Whatever. The dream's got nothing to do with religion."

"You sure about that."

"I want my friends to be searching for me the same way I'm trying to locate them. It's possible, right? I mean I have the name of the place they're headed to, but it's still possible they might have come back to the theater and seen the note we left them. I know you think it was stupid, the time I found the spray paint that worked, to scrawl my name on the wall, but at least it was something."

Abe stayed silent. He handed off the canteen, offering Eric a drink of water.

"Thanks." He took a generous sip, and some of the cool fluid trickled out of the corner of his mouth and on to his shirt.

When Eric returned it, the older man shoved the bottle into a duffle. "Ready to get out of Dodge?"

"Yes, sir."

"Then let's do another sweep before heading out."

He ran through the camp one last time, stomping

out the fire, working next to Abe to pack up the last bits.

When the ground was barren, and Eric headed toward the road, Abe placed a hand on his arm.

Abe's grip tightened around the hunting parka he'd commandeered from a local store.

"God sends us messages in some interesting ways. You need to be ready to listen."

"It's too early to discuss religion. How about we talk breakfast. I'm starving." Eric dismissed the comment.

Abe had done so much for him, but the older man's religious views, ones they often debated for hours on end, were hard to endure this early.

"Spoken like a youth."

He nodded even though he didn't appreciate the comment.

It had been a quiet night other than a strange dream and he hoped the day would be similar. He didn't want an argument first thing.

The hike began. It would be hours before Eric or Abe stopped and searched for something to eat from a house along the route. While he and the older man carried some supplies, it was easier to forage along the route, not that there was a clear picture of where to go. Eric hoped to remedy that by searching for maps and atlases at every stop.

When he found one, he studied the roads and highways, but during the trek had little time. Abe liked to keep moving.

Today, he didn't feel like talking. And silence dominated except for bird songs and squirrels preparing for winter.

With the maps safely tucked in his pack Eric began to wonder if there had to be something better than living on the road. He hoped finding his brother would lead him to that.

Life can't be enduring hardship until death. Could it? Surviving the attack in the movie theater must be significant. There must be a reason for it. and something more waits for me. Wait, am I buying into Abe's religious views? Crap.

He trudged on, interspersing long hikes with interval runs, and some impromptu training. He felt like a pirate when he and Abe parried on top of the charred, deteriorated cars rooted to the ground thanks to flat tires whose plastic had melted into the asphalt

The landscape remained free from the undead. He plodded onward, meandering through the woods, across highways and secondary roadways, all the time yearning to study the maps and atlases he'd gathered. He hiked as he had done every day since waking in the movie theater.

Tonight would be different, he promised himself. *With the maps, I can form a plan.*

He was thankful to Abe for being alive and searching for his family, but Abe had taught him to stay on the move. Dumb luck had helped the two of them avoid large nests of Streakers.

Luck might be running out if my dream's real.

5

STAINS

A black crow squawked from a high rooftop, but otherwise nothing moved inside or outside the deteriorating, uninhabited skeletons of buildings, each falling, day by day, into further ruin. No matter how many months passed, blood stains lingered on the doors, the walls, the floors of the homes Eric scavenged with Abe.

Eric wiped the pencil he'd taken from a home yesterday and tried unsuccessfully to rid it of the stain but couldn't. He'd ticked off another month in his journal. Two months and no sign of Billy. Abe avoided places humans might linger, and Eric could help but feel like the last two souls on earth.

Eric stomach still ached with hunger. Abe stood and repacked the canteen. Eric dropped the expired granola bar wrapper to the ground and followed Abe into the neighborhood.

The charred remains of houses had nothing left to scavenge. Block by block Eric and the older man traveled what had once barely been considered the town.

Decay, more than anything else, prevails.

Eric studied a paper map as they hiked the deserted streets and made their way to a clump of sad houses. He negotiated the litter-filled sidewalk, slowly and cautiously, avoiding stepping on glass, holding a discussion, or doing anything to draw the attention of Streakers.

A line on the map jumped out at him, and he contemplated a route he hadn't considered. Preoccupied with the black line of highway that would take him to Chincoteague, Virginia, he missed seeing the metal pipe in front of his feet. He stumbled, kicking the pipe into the street where it smashed into the burnt-out hull of a car. The last note of a metallic symphony rose into the air.

Abe sent him the evil eye.

Eric turned the corner and death stood waiting.

Death's extremely unattractive, Eric thought.

The zombie, clad in the remnants of black pants and a faded, blood-stained lime-colored T-shirt, waddled. It stunk of guts and bowels, worse than week-old roadkill.

The creature lifted its head and snorted, turning listless eyes in his direction. Eric raised the crowbar he held, and Abe stabbed his crescent shaped knife into the air. The Streaker, its body tattooed with decay, swayed and staggered.

Eric scrambled forward, ready to commence battle and to repay Abe for his kindness.

"Kid, let me handle this." Abe pushed in front of Eric.

"I'm good." Eric stepped closer to the evil.

Am I ready for this? He wondered. *I can't freeze.*

All the scars and wounds from last time, all caused by creatures such as this, grew sensitive—tingling even.

He had grown stronger and more deadly with Abe's help, but in many ways, he still doubts, and he hated that. Each morning hike in the sun left him more nourished than any food they found but the after-effects of what happened in the movie theater plagued his dreams. His body was strong, but doubt and fear had become his constant companions.

The undead closed the distance faster than Eric expected. Greasy black spittle arched out between the remains of lips. Talons ending with ghastly green, molding fingers, hooked bone and rotting flesh struck out to capture Eric's arm.

Eric's crowbar connected with the monster's jaw, shattering a few of the rotting teeth lingering in a stench-filled mouth. The corpse's mouth continued to crunch and chomp, unable to register pain from the blow of the crowbar, aching for the taste of human flesh.

Again, Eric aimed and slammed into the creature's skull.

The Streaker staggered back from the powerful blow.

"Careful," Abe warned, slicing at the creature, diverting its attention.

Snap. The crowbar cracked against the creature's neck. It staggered back a few steps and tumbled to the ground.

"You think I hit anything vital?" Eric asked. "I'm shocked it was so fast."

"Never underestimate them." Abe's eyes followed the zombie's every move.

Eric moved close, stood over the zombie that lay stunned on the ground, crowbar held above his head. Tightening his grip, he bashed at the undead that wiggled like a worm on the heated concrete. Grabbing the end of his weapon, Eric impaled the creature in the head.

The sickening crack of rotting bone and flesh accompanied the ooze of murky fluid.

Violence and rage coursed through him.

Eric repeated the downward strokes again and again.

Abe' grabbed his shoulder, jerking him away.

Eric staggered back. Glancing at the liquefied remains of the creature's skull, Eric turned away and gagged.

"It's dead now." Abe pointed at the puddle of a human corpse.

Eric gulped for breath.

"It feels good, getting rid of them." Abe patted his shoulder. "I understand but remember not to let the evil get in you." He paused, and studied Eric's face.

"I don't know what happened to me."

"You done good, taking on the undead. You're working through your fear."

"I don't know. I'm strong." Eric rolled his shoulders back. "I didn't freeze up and handled it better than I thought, at least until I couldn't stop."

Abe dragged Eric away. "Let's move and avoid the possibility of more lurking undead."

The next two hours of trekking proved uneventful. The further Eric and Abe traveled from the remnants of civilization the more comfortable he became, believing they had left most of the undead behind.

As society receded, Abe stopped along the route to scavenge a store or house, adding to his duffle bag an assortment of items: matches, clothes, and even a few overlooked dented cans of food.

This delay irked Eric, who wanted above all else to find the elusive inn.

6

A PATH

The picture still hung on the wall, but the image had faded and blood splattered the glass. Eric straightened the frame, staring at the boy, close to his age and his sister, years younger, who sat in front of smiling parents.

The personal stuff always bothers me the most.

After ensuring no Streakers resided inside, Eric turned away from Abe, leaving him to scavenge through the basement and kitchen. Eric climbed the steps to tackle the upstairs and attic.

He hoped to find another map, his collection growing. They grounded him to the past and were his hope for the future.

The farmhouse perched in desolation on a hill. The nearest neighbor miles away. That was usually better for them. When people were far from services, they planned and prepared ahead. They couldn't run downtown for a cup of coffee.

Eric heard Abe pulling out drawers and opening cabinets in the kitchen. They weren't the first here, but they were often still able to find hidden stashes others overlooked. Abe was methodical and taught Eric to be the same.

The stairs dumped him in a long corridor leading to three bedrooms and a bathroom. All the doors were open. He'd already made sure the area was clear. When he'd gone into the last bedroom, he'd come across the decayed carcass of a dog lying next to his owner who, for whatever reason hadn't risen as a Streaker. There was little left but bone, scavengers having had ample time to pick the dead clean. Eric almost balled like a baby but managed to stem the flow of tears by punching his fist against the palm of his opposite hand. Sometimes, the pain of missing his family flew through him like a tornado, destructive and devastating.

He entered the first room, once decorated with superhero and movie posters. These had withered to the floor, for the most part little more than shredded scrap paper. There was a shelf of books, and Eric reached out to select one. He cradled a graphic novel, skimmed the pages and returned it. He did the same for another book, and then shoved a copy of *The Lord of the Flies* in his backpack. He'd skipped the novel during freshman year of high school, not exactly a reader back then. He thought it might be worth giving it a go now.

The teen must have been an artist. Decaying sketch pads had molded to the point where it was hard to tell what the images had once been. Eric plucked one from the floor and flipped through it. Most of the images were incomprehensible. One one of the last pages, a monster lurked. Undead and eerily familiar. The face of the boy's mom stared back at him. Eric dropped the sketch pad to the floor.

He stepped on each of the floorboards seeing if any were loose and searched the closet for hidden panels. At the end of the world, people hid things in odd places. His search provided some clean clothes, a charcoal pencil, a backpack to keep his scarce personal belongings, and a pair of sneakers for his feet, only a couple sizes too big.

After he finished searching, he moved on to the next bedroom, the sister. Again, waves of sadness shuddered through Eric. The shelves and floor were covered with broken and toppled awards and ribbons. She'd been a ballet dancer, a horseback rider, and part of the 4-H. Most likely, now she was a walking corpse.

Her room provided little. He moved on to the master suite. He covered the corpse with a sheet, unable to gaze at man and dog. The box full of jewelry and money was useless. Eric went through the closets and layered his out with a red plaid flannel shirt. There was a winter coat hanging, but Eric decided it was too bulky and not worth the extra weight. He went through the room, step by step, checking ever nook and cranny for items of use. He hated having to reach under the mattress, almost didn't with the corpse on it, but didn't want to disappoint Abe.

On the shelves were more books, mostly molded romances, but there were a few travel books. He flipped through one about Virginia is for Lovers. In the best inns for romance, the High Point was listed. He had an address now in addition to the town. He had plenty of maps to figure out the route.

He ran to tell Abe.

After combing the house, collecting their supplies Eric strode down the road next to Abe, his mind fluttering with the possibility of seeing his friends soon. He ought to be bone-weary now that evening setting in. Between the fight, scavenging, and the hard day's trek, he should be falling down. Instead, excitement coursed through him.

A woodsy area off the side of the highway offered solace and Eric helped Abe set camp as late evening approached. Having scored matches, the Eric and Abe set out to collect wood and risked a larger than normal fire, heating cans of soup, infused with a random can of jalapenos.

"I don't usually break out the dinnerware, but since you're here, I need to use my extra mug all the time. You're in a good mood. We might as well celebrate your find today."

Eric grabbed a jalapeno and popped it in his mouth. Seconds later, his sputtering cough echoed throughout the campsite. "Hot. Hot." Eric shoveled the liquid meal into his mouth and fanned his mouth with a hand.

Abe's laughter rumbled in the surrounding air.

"This is a feast compared to some of the things I've eaten in the past. Once, I scored six cans of beans and lived on them for two weeks. At least there's some diversity tonight."

"It will be better at the inn for everyone," Eric sipped to soup. "Life will be normal again."

Abe shook his head. "Get used to the new normal. Don't expect too much. You might be disappointed when we get to the inn. You don't know if it was inhabitable, if your friends made it, or what they'd be able to accomplish."

Eric covered his head with the hood of the sweatshirt. "They made it. I have no doubts."

Abe belched loudly, his empty plate hitting the ground with a dull thud. "Your scars should be almost healed up by now. How are you feeling?"

Eric pushed up the sleeve of his sweatshirt.

The older man inspected Eric's arm. "Your arm looks great. I know it's been, what now, almost three months, but you're healed, and I'd swear to God you've grown two inches and put on twenty pounds. When I think back to the day I found you in the movie theater, I'm still in shock you survived. I sat up that first night thinking I'd have to put a bullet in your head before morning. You were a mess."

Eric inspected his arm. Light scars like feathers still crisscrossed them, puffy and pink, but fully healed "I'm happy you didn't shoot me."

"You're a freaking miracle. This has to be a sign."

"What are you saying? A sign of what?"

" A sign from God." Abe reached out and patted Eric's arm. "You not only survived but healed."

"I'm a quick healer."

"It's all clear now. We need to stay together."

"I thought we already decided to stay together."

Eric scratched his head and realized he needed a bath.

"This is different. I think God has bigger plans for us. We have to stay together and wait for the miracle or at least a sign pointing us in that direction."

7

HIGHWAY TO HELL

Eric made another mark on the ratty backpack with a black sharpie scavenged from the remains of a corner store more than a week ago. The numerous hand-drawn lines, previously etched, were already fading and hard to read through the layers of grime. The pen itself, old and dry was about to give out, but each line was important to Eric. They were one day closer.

Eric and Abe had traveled for three months. Lacking a calendar, Eric guessed the month to be November or December. Cooler temperatures had arrived, bringing darkness early each day. He was angry at himself for all the detours and mistakes he'd made on the trip before collected the maps and finding the town. He'd been so weak at the start too, unable to travel more than a few miles each day.

I didn't matter now. I'll be there soon now that I have the information on the inn and the maps to show me the way.

Eric and Abe set off in the early hours of the morning, the sun not yet on the horizon. Abe kept up a grueling pace the entire day and spoke little. Every attempt by Eric to start a conversation provoked grunts and one-word answers. Eric wondered if Abe was worried about meeting everyone at the inn. The more excited Eric became, the more Abe's mood soured.

By nightfall, Eric staggered over the rusted cans and stones littering the road. to find some strength, he plied a granola bar from the pocket from his jeans, noting the date of expiration only a few months prior. He took a bite. It tasted like a brick but he was happy for the meager rations.

Abe peered over his shoulder. "You drunk boy?"

"If only that were a possibility."

"Liquor's around, but it's a vice. You need to stay sharp."

"Still, I'd like to try a good whiskey once. My dad used to always talk about it when he splurged in a restaurant." A rush of memories left him quiet.

Abe stopped and faced him. "If we're still together when you turn eighteen, I'll find a bottle for you."

There'd be no party at eighteen or twenty-one. "I'll be lucky to survive into my twenties. Honestly, I'd be happy for a can of coke or a cup of coffee. Boiled river water is getting old." Soda and juice had become faded memories, the thought of them made his mouth water. They'd once found an orange tree ripe with fruit in warmer days and had gorged themselves. With colder weather upon them, nothing would bear fruit until spring.

There were rare times Abe and he would stumble upon exotic and not so exotic brands of liquid refreshment. Abe had let him try a thimble full of coffee liqueur once. He'd come across a sports drink in someone's hoard. The refreshing taste mixed with so many bitter memories, Eric wasn't sure he enjoyed it. Canteen to his lips, Eric gulped the water and slogged along, hoping Abe would end the trek soon.

Half an hour later, Abe pointed out a secluded spot for the night and started a fire. Their most recent camp was hidden in the woods next to the guardrail, obscuring the smoke from the small fire. They had a view of car hoods on the highway below, the battered reminder of previous existence. From the perch on the hill, sheltered by the tree, they had the vantage point.

Eric assembled the tent and enjoyed his survival

rations meal. He'd been lucky to stumble across tubs of Traveler's Stew with a 25-year shelf life. The mixture bubbled in the pan as the fire sputtered under it, the smell making Eric's stomach whine in anticipation.

Dividing the contents, Eric poured half into a mess-kit bowl and handed it to Abe. He slurped his stew directly from the pan. The two spoke little, sitting in silence born of their companionship.

"You okay on first shift?" Eric rose and stretched. "I'm exhausted."

Abe put his empty plate on the ground and cleared his throat. "Get some shut you're your time will come soon enough."

Slurping the last pieces of stew, Eric rose and cleaned his mess kit. Inside the tent, he unrolled the sleeping bag, falling onto it exhausted. An uneventful night passed with Eric sitting guard for a few hours, tending the fire and trying to read the maps in the darkness. Abe woke before the sunrise, grabbed a canteen of water, took a long gulp, and began disassembling the camp. Before they left, Abe had Eric open the maps and sit with him. Eric watched as the older man examined them.

"They'll be lots of supplies along the coastline. Access to resources too"

"But we're so close." Eric hated the whine that joined his words.

"You have to be prepared for anything. We need to bulk up."

"Can't we do that after we find the inn?" Eric flicked the tangled, blond hair out of his eyes.

"One stop." Abe stood. "That's all I'm asking."

Eric had organized the last part of the trek thanks to his maps. At first, he'd been angry with himself for taking so long to figure out how helpful the maps would be, but they were close now and he was ready for the reunion. He never passed up collecting a map or atlas now, even it it was for a different state or country. You never knew what might happen, and his collection had grown rather large.

After studying the maps and completing the breakdown of the camp, Eric joined Abe on the road.

"We agree to make one more detour," Abe marched along the road. They maneuvered around the cars. There was a pile up of them ahead, but it was off the side and easy to skirt around.

"If we must." Eric grumbled.

They continued their trek. Eric unzipped his parka when the winter sun permeated the layers of his clothing. They were a few hours into their daily hike, and Abe had yet to stop for breakfast, but at least there hadn't been any new training this morning.

Abe pointed off the side of the road. "Smoke."

"What does that mean?"

"Could be a camp or a natural fire. We should check it out."

Eric shrugged. "What if it's people?"

"We leave them be and go our way."

"They've survived this long. They could be helpful."

"They could also kill us and take all our stuff." Abe moved to the side of the road, jumped the guardrail, and found a large rock outcrop. "Leave your pack here."

Eric dropped his gear and followed Abe toward the whisps of smoke.

The camp appeared deserted.

"The fire's almost out." Abe stamped on the dying fire. "Looks like some embers caught and that's why there's smoke, but all the woods burned down."

Eric surveyed the area. "People could still be around. They could be hunting or something."

Abe pointed to a crossbow. "Without gear? Something bad happened here and we shouldn't linger"

"What if someone's injured or in need of help."

"Not our problem." Abe see-sawed a knife out of

a log it had been embedded in and held it in his palm.

"Take everything useful."

Eric's mouth opened and closed. "What?"

"Come on." Abe started collecting supplies.

"What if they're alive and come back?"

"Then they were stupid to leave everything unattended, but believe me, they're not coming back."

Trudging along the highway, Eric swung the new hunting knife he'd found at the deserted camp site. The crossbow wacked his hip with every step. His pack weighed heavy on his shoulders, full of new supplies. He wondered what happened. The people were gone, but the camp seemed relatively new.

"I don't feel right about taking all their stuff." Eric swapped the blade from palm to palm.

"God works in mysterious ways." Abe peered over his shoulder. "He provided for us when we needed it."

"Doesn't seem right."

"Nothing about this situation is right from the time it started. People believed global warming was fake. A scam liberal fabricated. They didn't want to stop spending money and buying useless junk. Consumerism killed the planet. Technology killed humanity."

"Is this what you consider light dinner conversation?"

"There's no such thing as easy conversations these days. I'm trying to teach you something, Kid."

"I beginning to take offense at the nickname. I've proven myself many times over. I'd like to be called Wolverine or young Wolverine if you want to pretend to be my mentor. We could always call you Yoda and me young Skywalker. That's a light conversation, determining our new nicknames."

"We can tackle new nicknames tomorrow." Abe ranted. "You need to understand this. Computers and technology caused an epidemic loss of spirituality. It doesn't matter what God you pray to, at the time of the pandemic, no one was praying. Technology and science led us to our own destruction, not some virus."

"I'm not following." Eric scratched at his chin scruff.

I'm more interested in finding a razor than listening to a lecture.

"God had a plan for what's left of humanity and now you're part of it. It was my destiny to run into you. He's chosen us for some reason, and we have a responsibility to make this horrible new world livable. Whether it's defeating the Streakers or starting over, it's our time to make the changes."

"That's a lot of pressure to put on yourself. And to put on me. How about we just try and stay alive another couple days."

Abe twisted, walking backwards along the straight road. "No such luck. Think about your past. The oil and gas that heated our houses and the electricity used to run our computers killed the planet, but humans didn't care. They kept wasting these precious, God-given resources. We wanted more and our gluttony destroyed us. We destroyed the paradise God gave us and now He seeks revenge."

Eric stopped and stood rooted in the middle of the road. "Where is this coming from, Abe? I've never heard you speak like this before."

"I've had a lot of time to consider this since we met. The two of us have a chance to start over. By putting everything technological behind us, by living simply and of the earth, we'll be able to rebuild."

"I get the living simply part. I'm just not buying the wrath of God stuff."

"Think of what was happening prior to the Streakers. The world endured tornadoes, hurricanes, blizzards, and droughts. People caused of the problem but refused to change so God demanded it."

Eric relented and began to walk. "What now?"

"I'm not sure."

Eric was uneasy. He'd didn't like the one-sided

nature of the conversation, let alone the content. He drew out a different worn map, tattered and full of holes and rips, the map displayed black tick marks of the towns he walked through on the way to the inn. A black squiggly line indicated the route they were walking.

"We're near the Chesapeake Bay." He pointed to Chincoteague. "You want to stop here."

Abe eyed the map, examined the road ahead of them. "There's a lot of wilderness around, but it also looks touristy too. It's a good location for supplies but we can hopefully avoid masses of Streakers."

Eric trailed behind Abe on the gently winding asphalt, broken glass and rusted cans, crunching under brown work boots. He pondered his new skills. He'd turned into an efficient killer.

So engrossed in thought, it took Eric a moment to recognize the engine ricocheting through the empty air on a road devoid of any other sounds of life.

There was a mechanical sputter and cough.

Today, the highway appeared no safer than the wilderness surging around them, growing over the guardrails and through the cracks of the no longer well-traveled expressways.

8

THE DEVIL DRIVES A VAN

"Move." Abe shouted and grabbed Eric's arm, hauling him along the road until they came to a dilapidated car, burnt out and prone on its side. The remains of a door jutted towards the heavens. Abe motioned him toward it and Eric crawled in, the cold of the metal burning his palms. He made room for Abe. Jammed together, Eric's cumbersome gear pinched his back as they hid from an unknown enemy. Eric tried to quiet his loud and ragged breathing.

A worn out, graffiti covered van slowed as it neared Abe and Eric. It stuttered to a stop. A large, scruffy man, heavily bearded and armed with an ax emerged from the gloomy interior of its back door. On his belt, the metal of a knife reflected the sun. Covering his free hand, brass knuckles weighed upon gloved fingers. Four gloved fingers. The man was missing his thumb. He scanned the road before marching a few steps. Bending down, he grabbed something off the pavement.

"Shit." Eric whispered.

"What is it?"

"It's my map! It was in my back pocket. It must have fallen out."

"It's just garbage on the road." Abe whispered back.

"Maybe." Eric wasn't convinced.

The man surveyed the empty highway around him. He pivoted and Eric hoped he would return to the battered van. Instead, he called to those inside.

"Jones, Frank, get out here. Let's search the area. I saw something." The man's voice was louder than needed. The stranger wanted Eric and Abe to hear, his smile predatorial.

I'm the prey.

Two additional men exited the van, both similar in appearance and as heavily armed as the first, savagery in every step. One brandished a knife as he lumbered away from the van. They fanned out across the road, checking every abandoned vehicle. Each empty shell of a car or truck brought them closer to Eric and Abe.

"We can't let them find us trapped in the car. We won't be able to fight back," whispered Abe.

"Maybe they're really nice guys."

"Wishful thinking", he huffed. "These guys will kill us for our supplies."

"What do we do?"

"We fight for our lives, Kid. It's us or them," Abe murmured in hushed tones. "You ready?"

Eric nodded, wiggling out of his backpack and following Abe as he slid from the car. Eric did the same. Once out, he crouched by the side of the vehicle, leaning against the burnt-out door and into the jagged metal pieces that pinched his back.

He waited.

One of the strangers moved close.

Abe, Bowie knife in hand, rushed at him. Abe rammed the stranger, toppling into a heap of limbs on the ground. Punches and kicks flew. Eric remained immobile, unable to differentiate a winner from a loser. Out of the corner of his eye, he noticed a blur of movement. A man with a thick beard and one eye swollen shut cornered him.

Eric stood, unsure of what to do. He fought Streakers, not humans. The man standing here, the one who first exited the van, appearing taller, huskier, and much more menacing. Then, he dropped the ax and put his knife back in the belt loop of his jeans.

Should I try to reason with hm? Explain why Abe and I are out here and that I'm searching for my brother?

"I won't need this with you, too pretty with all the long hair." He chuckled. "Might be some use for you."

The stranger smiled and without warning, threw a punch. Eric reacted a second too late. The punch hit his cheek. The brass knuckles on the man's other hand met Eric's ribs, doubling him over. violently expelling the air from his lungs.

Eric fell to one knee, wanted to drop to the ground, pain radiating from his stomach, mind blurry, but forced himself upright just in time to block the next blow.

The fear twisting inside him morphed, spurning something new. He used the pain and turmoil, the loss of his brother and family, the anger from the endless search, and his fear to find his courage.

Eric wanted to live.

Courage fueled his soul, but the months of training with Abe helped in other, equally as important ways.

Staring at the stranger, eyeing the remains of food in his beard and shifty, single bloodshot eye, Eric threw a punch. He'd aimed for the man's greasy chin but hit the stranger's shoulder. The man staggered backward.

"You little shit." He lurched forward, but Eric blocked the blow aimed at his face. He ducked the next one, brass knuckles swinging over his head.

Eric countered with a couple weak punches of his own, nothing connecting.

His assailant plunged forward, delivering a powerful punch to Eric's ribs. The stranger rammed Eric, but Eric locked his arms around the man's paunchy middle in a bear hug, refusing to drop like grass under the blade of a lawnmower.

Breaking the hold, the stranger stepped back and threw another punch. Eric blocked the brunt of it, locking the hand between his own two. He pushed back, but the man sidestepped to remain upright.

Eric released his hold and attacked, knuckles stinging as soft skin met the metal buttons of the man's jacket before the cartilage of the man's nose.

Three solid punches. Blood leaked from his assailant's nose, dripping on an already stained shirt. Eric delivered a hard punch and the man's lip split under the weight of his knuckles. His jabs grew more determined.

The man's cheek bone crunched, and his hands flew up to his face.

Eric didn't care and aimed a blow at his abdomen.

The stranger fell, a whimper escaping his lips as his head struck the pavement.

Eric swiveled, searching for Abe who was grappling with one of the other men from the van. Eric ran to help.

A serrated knife, glinting in the light, posed inches in front of his abdomen, cut off his advance. An evil face sneered from behind the blade.

"You like to fight, do you?" The stranger asked. His smile revealed brown, decaying teeth. The blade twirled in his hand, shifty eyes glancing at the body on the ground.

The attacker studied Eric. A smile stretched across scabby lips. "You don't look like much." He spat on Eric's boots, "but you brought Big Ed down. Maybe there's more to you than pretty looks."

Eric met the eyes of his opponent and didn't see anything human remaining.

The man leered and hefted his substantial bulk and all-too-sharp knife closer to Eric.

"Shall we dance?" The stranger slashed at Eric who fumbled to withdraw his own knife from his belt.

He withdrew it awkwardly, clumsy and incompetent, but recovered enough to cast away the knife with his own.

Eric dodged the first thrusts, but his opponent was seasoned, more skilled. Streaks of red criss-crossed his arms and chest. Although not deadly wounds, each new cut brought pain, making Eric unsure. The continued parry wearied him to the point that no amount of adrenaline could boost his stamina.

He fought the idea of surrender.

Lashing out, the assailant nicked Eric's arm with the knife once again and blood seeped from a deep gash. An uncomfortable spark, as if embers from the fire had scorched his skin, launched Eric into action.

This must end, he thought. *I must finish it, or I'll be dead.*

Striking out again, allowing Eric no rest, the stranger's knife etched another trail of red across his arm. The man charged, knife high, aiming the killing stroke.

Eric saw his attacker's weakness and dodged the high blade. The weapon slashed at his scalp, barely missing.

Keeping his weapon low, Eric found the stranger's gut. He hated the give and take of the soft flesh as he stabbed. A slick red wetness covered the man's stomach and legs and leaked onto Eric's

Anything in it to keep the two women alive was worth salvaging.

Abe and Eric piled the dead men's bodies in the middle of the highway and set them aflame to ensure the men, newly dead, would not return as Streakers. Eric kept watch to make sure the noise, smoke, and fire did not attract any curious, hungry, or unwelcome visitors. He stood, back turned away from Abe as the smell of burning flesh turned his stomach.

A single tear trickled from the corner of his eye.

When the remains of the bodies smoldered, little more than ash and bone, Eric returned to offer the women the discarded clothing.

"Take this." He handed a ripped and strained t-shirt to one of the women. "Put this on." She took it and did nothing with it other than to hold it.

"Put in on."

Her eyes remained unfocused.

"Can you put it on?" When he reached out to her, the woman flinched and recoiled. Eric took the t-shirt back and gently placed it over the woman's head, carefully threaded each arm through the sleeves. He continued to dress the women in the clothing taken from the dead men like a parent would dress a toddler. Although most was much too big, Eric was resourceful and made the clothing fit with the aid of belts, string, and shoelaces.

hands. Skin puckered and sighed as he removed the knife the last time.

Eyes wide, the man fell.

Eric stood speechless.

I killed someone. I should feel something.

He dropped to his knees, attempted to stand, and fell again.

Abe came over and put a hand on his shoulder.

"It had to be done. It was them or us."

Eric nodded, "I know.".

"Let's check out the van." Abe ordered Eric into action. "We'll use it until it runs out of gas. We deserve a free ride today."

The two opened the side door and unleashed the overpowering smell of unwashed human flesh.

Eric stared in horror at two women, gagged and bound naked in the back of the vehicle. Little more than skin and bone.

"Shit." Abe's curse lingered in the air between them.

"What is this?"

"I wish I could spare you. This is the proof you need to see to know what people are like now. Help me set them free."

Eric and Abe peered into the cavernous recesses of the back of the van. Two women, limp and silent, sat bound together. Eric worked to untie them, but even free from the ropes cutting into their flesh and led from the van, they stood, unmoving. At the side of the road, the women waited, unspeaking.

"What's wrong with them?" Eric asked.

"Everything. They've suffered. The abuse they lived through by those men would kill most people."

"How can we help them?"

"We can't there's nothing we can do."

"What?" Eric balked at the cold edge to Abe's voice. "What do you mean we're not going to help them?"

"They'll drain our already limited supplies. They can hardly stand. We set them free."

"You helped me."

"It was different. I saw your resilience and look what an asset you've become. You're the chosen one." Abe pointed to the skeletal women "They-are liabilities."

The women stared as if deaf and uncomprehending, making no attempt to run or cover their nakedness. The two were little more than zombies.

"I was nearly dead. You still let me come with you. We can't just leave them here."

"We have to. Do you want to find your friends and family? It will never happen if we have to care for them. It will take weeks nursing them back to health just so they'd be able to march each day."

Eric's gaze shifted between the women an
"We have to do something for them."

"There's nothing to do but let them freedom."

"I'm not leaving them in the middle of th naked and starving. I can't do it. Even if th come with us, we have to help them stay aliv

"Kid, it's a waste of time and of our stuff

"I'm staying with them."

Abe squinted, his lips drawing into a sc Let's get them some clothes, supplies and offer you'll get from me."

"Fine," Eric agreed, face radiating turmoil. His desire to do more for the w obvious in every angry movement.

Eric stomped over to his map, wrest ground, making sure it was secure in hi

He returned to the van and slamm He heard Abe as he searched the dead them of clothing and collecting wha blood soaked. Along with the weapon pocketknife, some money, and a fad little girl. Everything of value was makeshift pile. It reminded Eric o pictures from school long ago, the clothing and shoes.

At least this pile was assembled

hands. Skin puckered and sighed as he removed the knife the last time.

Eyes wide, the man fell.

Eric stood speechless.

I killed someone. I should feel something.

He dropped to his knees, attempted to stand, and fell again.

Abe came over and put a hand on his shoulder.

"It had to be done. It was them or us."

Eric nodded, "I know.".

"Let's check out the van." Abe ordered Eric into action. "We'll use it until it runs out of gas. We deserve a free ride today."

The two opened the side door and unleashed the overpowering smell of unwashed human flesh.

Eric stared in horror at two women, gagged and bound naked in the back of the vehicle. Little more than skin and bone.

"Shit." Abe's curse lingered in the air between them.

"What is this?"

"I wish I could spare you. This is the proof you need to see to know what people are like now. Help me set them free."

Eric and Abe peered into the cavernous recesses of the back of the van. Two women, limp and silent, sat bound together. Eric worked to untie them, but even free from the ropes cutting into their flesh and led from the van, they stood, unmoving. At the side of the road, the women waited, unspeaking.

"What's wrong with them?" Eric asked.

"Everything. They've suffered. The abuse they lived through by those men would kill most people."

"How can we help them?"

"We can't there's nothing we can do."

"What?" Eric balked at the cold edge to Abe's voice. "What do you mean we're not going to help them?"

"They'll drain our already limited supplies. They can hardly stand. We set them free."

"You helped me."

"It was different. I saw your resilience and look what an asset you've become. You're the chosen one." Abe pointed to the skeletal women "They-are liabilities."

The women stared as if deaf and uncomprehending, making no attempt to run or cover their nakedness. The two were little more than zombies.

"I was nearly dead. You still let me come with you. We can't just leave them here."

"We have to. Do you want to find your friends and family? It will never happen if we have to care for them. It will take weeks nursing them back to health just so they'd be able to march each day."

Eric's gaze shifted between the women and Abe. "We have to do something for them."

"There's nothing to do but let them have freedom."

"I'm not leaving them in the middle of the road, naked and starving. I can't do it. Even if they can't come with us, we have to help them stay alive."

"Kid, it's a waste of time and of our stuff."

"I'm staying with them."

Abe squinted, his lips drawing into a scowl. "Fine. Let's get them some clothes, supplies and food. Best offer you'll get from me."

"Fine," Eric agreed, face radiating his inner turmoil. His desire to do more for the women made obvious in every angry movement.

Eric stomped over to his map, wrestling it off the ground, making sure it was secure in his pocket.

He returned to the van and slammed through it. He heard Abe as he searched the dead men, stripping them of clothing and collecting what was not too blood soaked. Along with the weapons, Abe found a pocketknife, some money, and a faded picture of a little girl. Everything of value was organized in a makeshift pile. It reminded Eric of the Holocaust pictures from school long ago, the piles and piles of clothing and shoes.

At least this pile was assembled to help someone.

Anything in it to keep the two women alive was worth salvaging.

Abe and Eric piled the dead men's bodies in the middle of the highway and set them aflame to ensure the men, newly dead, would not return as Streakers. Eric kept watch to make sure the noise, smoke, and fire did not attract any curious, hungry, or unwelcome visitors. He stood, back turned away from Abe as the smell of burning flesh turned his stomach.

A single tear trickled from the corner of his eye.

When the remains of the bodies smoldered, little more than ash and bone, Eric returned to offer the women the discarded clothing.

"Take this." He handed a ripped and strained t-shirt to one of the women. "Put this on." She took it but did nothing with it other than to hold it.

"Put in on."

Her eyes remained unfocused.

"Can you put it on?" When he reached out to her, the woman flinched and recoiled. Eric took the t-shirt back and gently placed it over the woman's head, carefully threaded each arm through the sleeves. He continued to dress the women in the clothing taken from the dead men like a parent would dress a toddler. Although most was much too big, Eric was resourceful and made the clothing work with the aid of belts, string, and shoelaces.